The Advent

Come In,
Zip! DISCARD

David
Milgrim

For Jake

Ready-to-Read

SIMON SPOTLIGHT

New York London Toronto Sydney New Delhi

Here is a list of all the words you will find in this book. Sound them out before you begin reading the story.

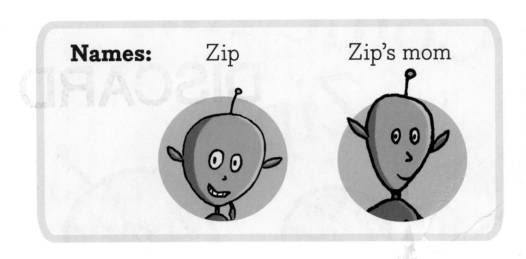

Names: Zip   Zip's mom

Word families:

"-ar"	→	car	far		
"-ay"	→	away	day	play	say
"-un"	→	fun	run	sun	

SIMON SPOTLIGHT
An imprint of Simon & Schuster Children's Publishing Division
1230 Avenue of the Americas, New York, New York 10020
This Simon Spotlight edition May 2020
Copyright © 2020 by David Milgrim
All rights reserved, including the right of reproduction in whole or in part in any form.
SIMON SPOTLIGHT, READY-TO-READ, and colophon are registered trademarks of Simon & Schuster, Inc.
For information about special discounts for bulk purchases, please contact Simon & Schuster Special Sales
at 1-866-506-1949 or business@simonandschuster.com.
Manufactured in the United States of America 0420 LAK
2 4 6 8 10 9 7 5 3 1
Library of Congress Control Number 2019952588
ISBN 978-1-5344-6564-0 (hc)
ISBN 978-1-5344-6563-3 (pbk)
ISBN 978-1-5344-6565-7 (eBook)

Sight words:

a	and	but	can	cannot
come	fast	fly	for	from
go	has	have	hear	in
is	me	more	not	now
see	so	than	the	we
you				

Bonus words:

bit	blow	done	faster	jet
night	outrun	roll	wind	zap
zaps				

Ready to go? Happy reading!

Don't miss the questions about the story
at the end of this book.

See Zip.

See Zip zap.

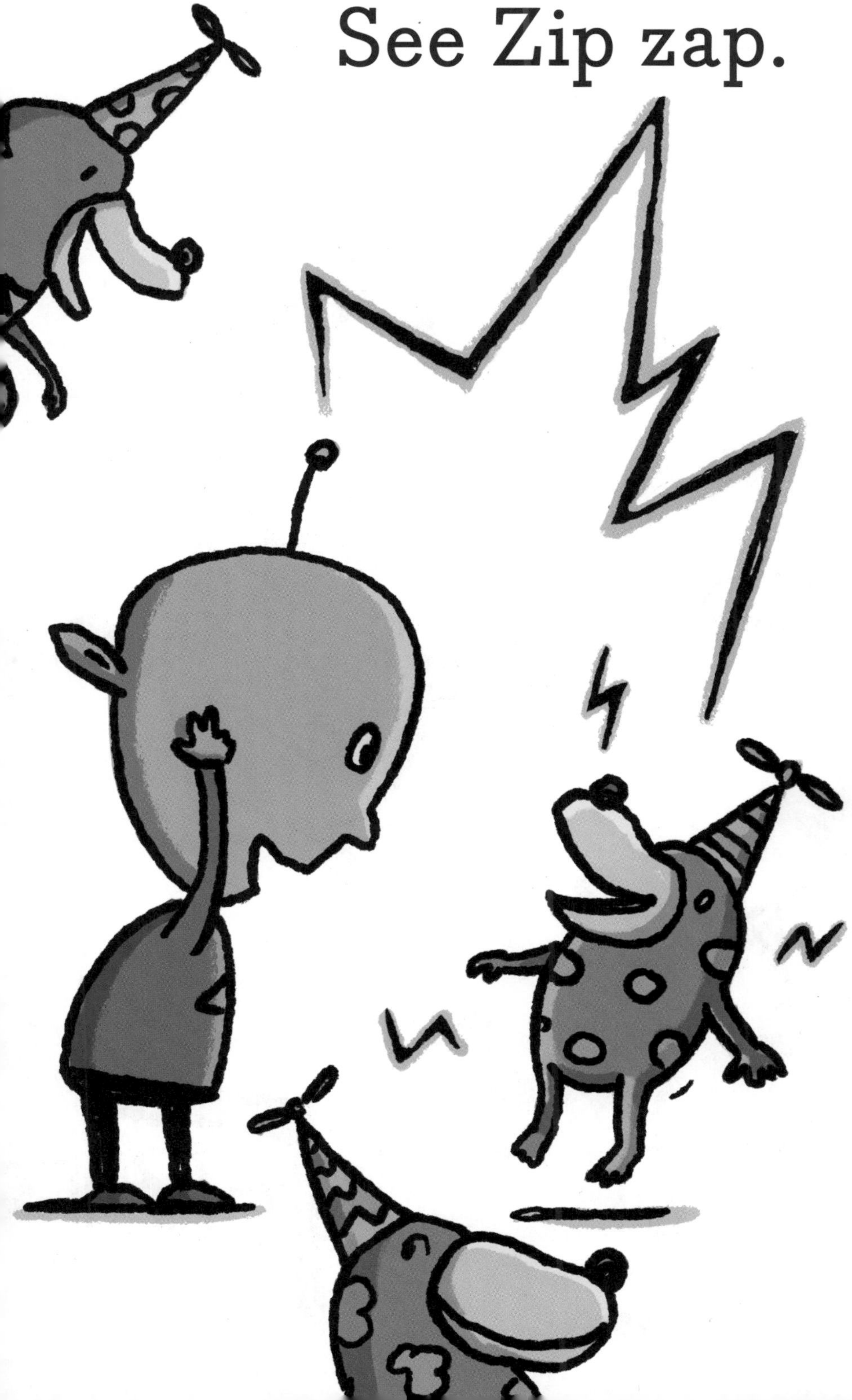

See Zip play.

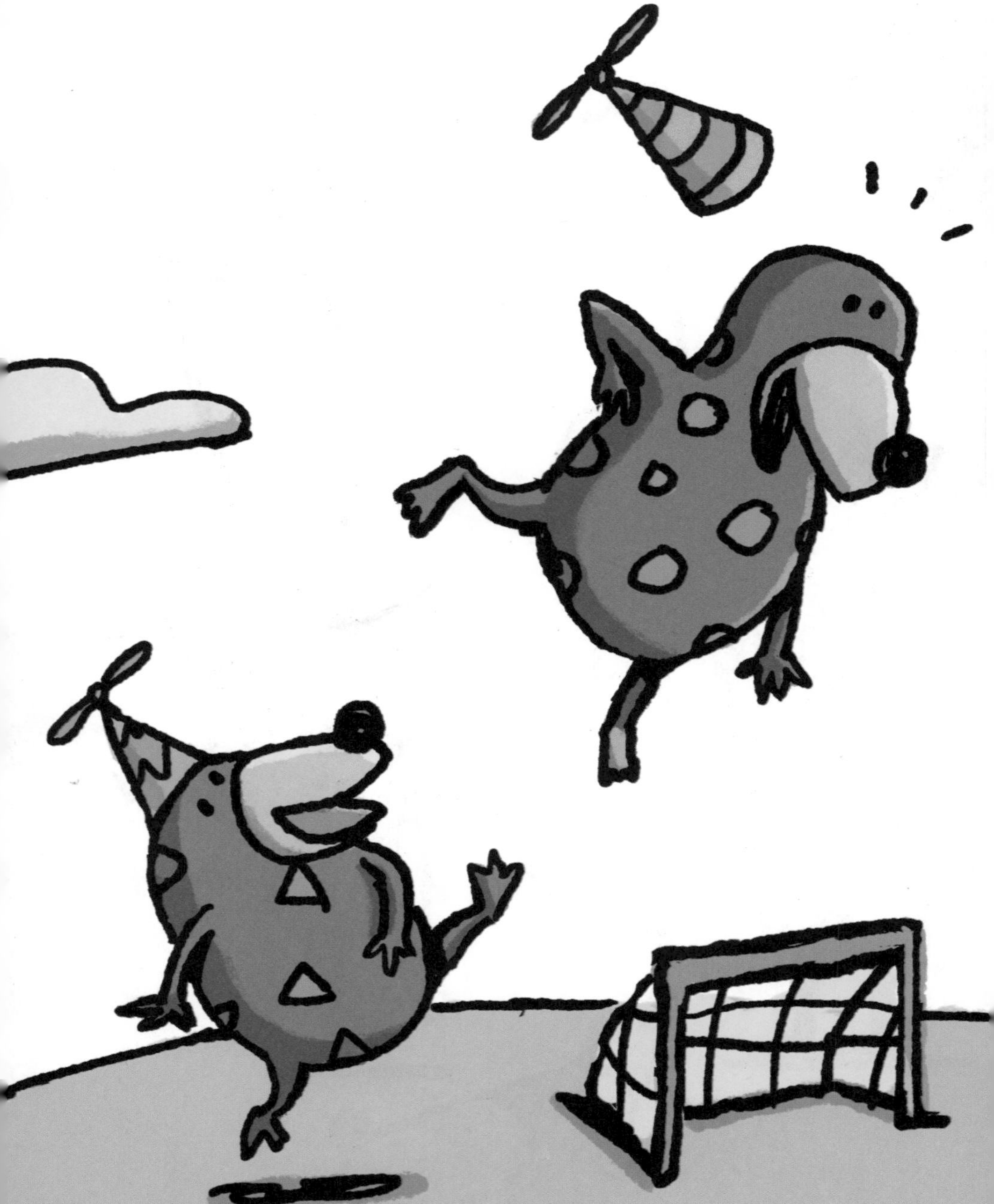

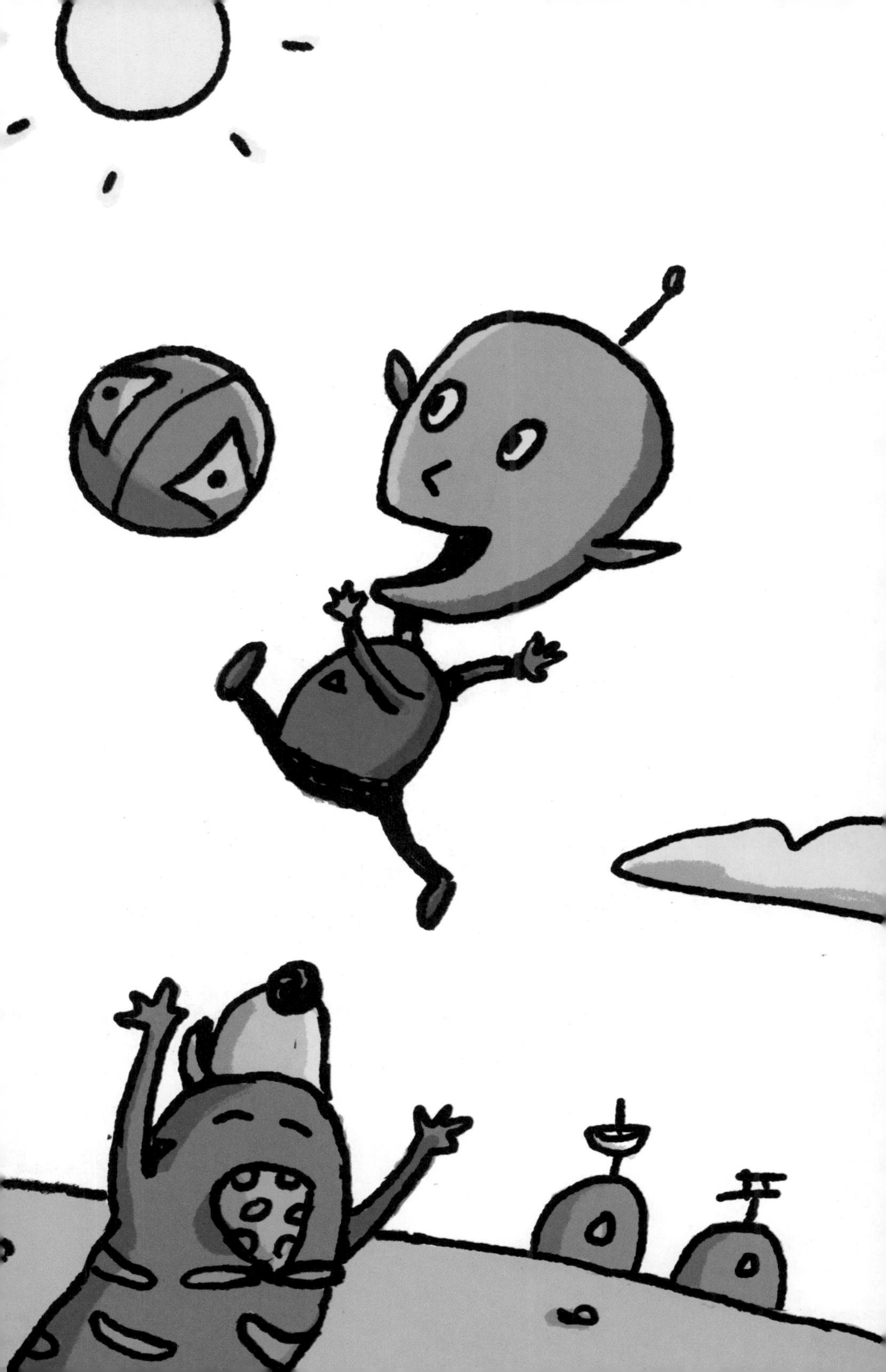

See Zip's mom.
See Zip's mom say,

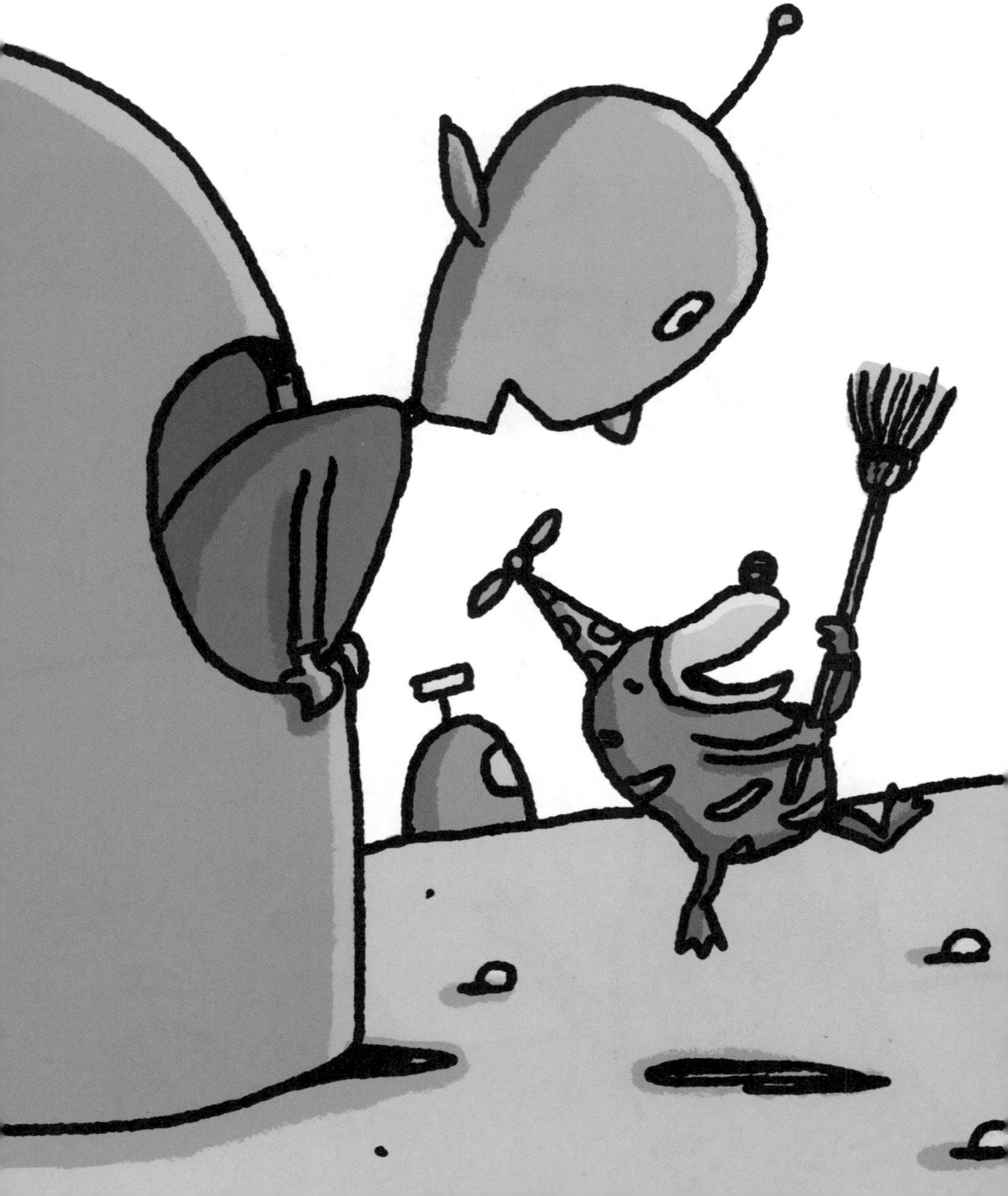

"Come in now, Zip,
in for the day."

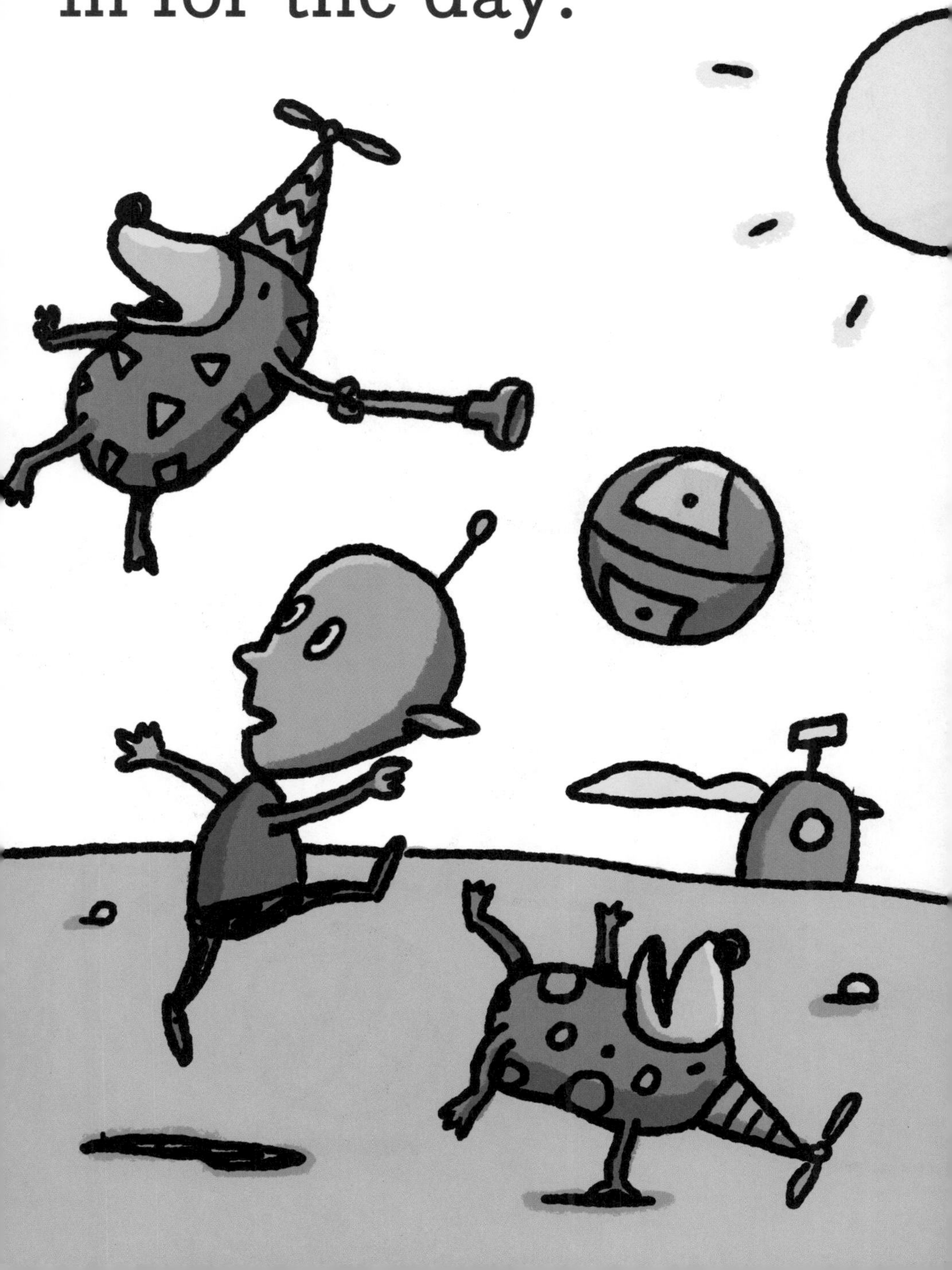

See Zip run.

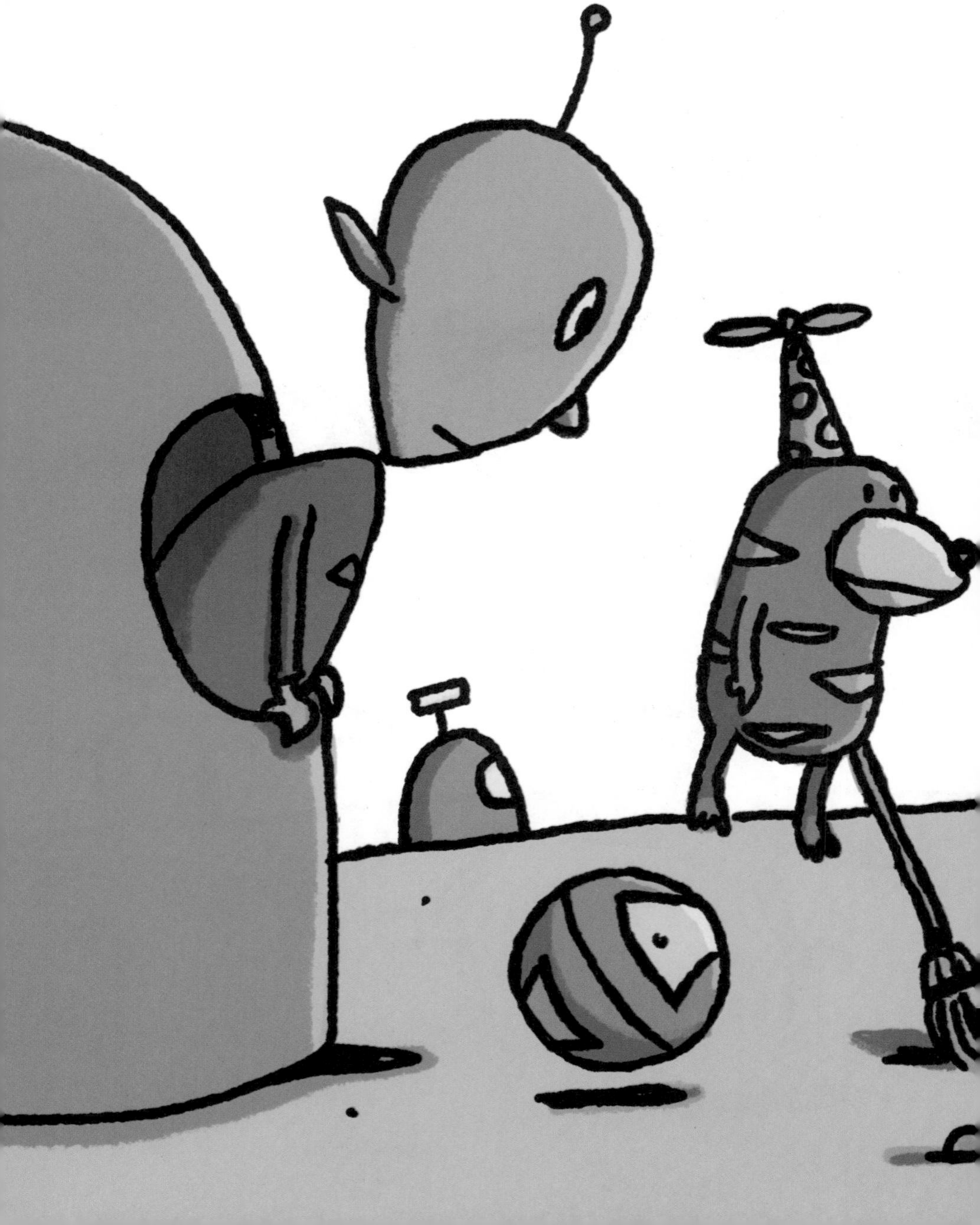

Run, run away.

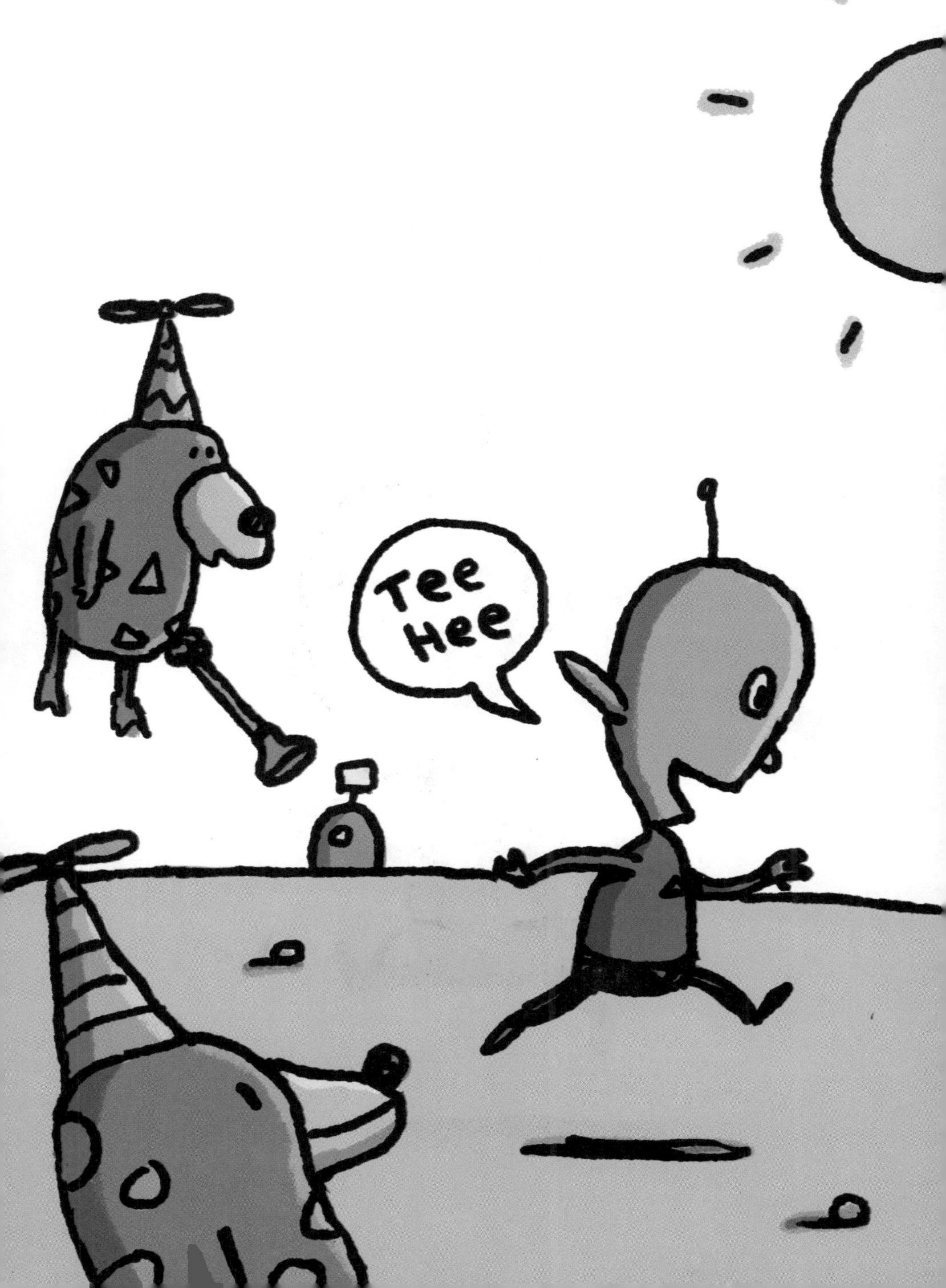
Tee Hee

"Not so fast,"
hear Zip's mom say.

"From me you cannot run away."

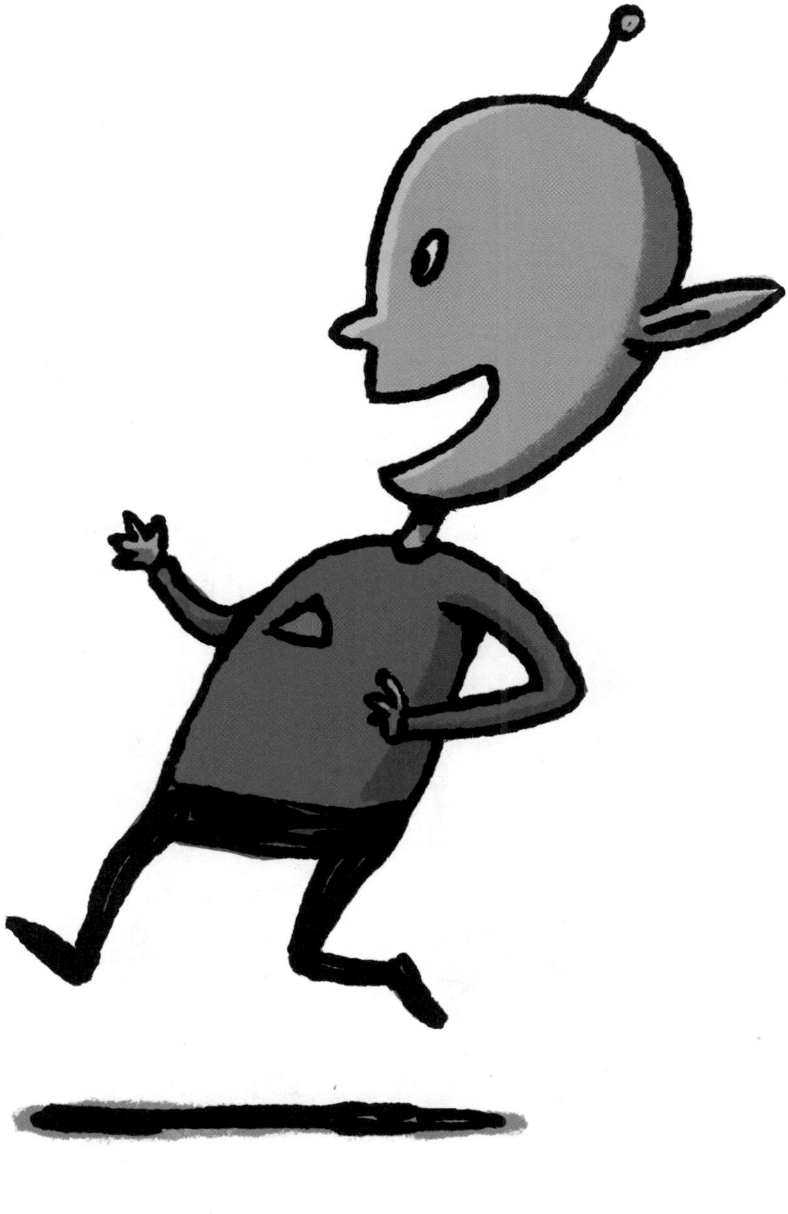

See Zip zap!

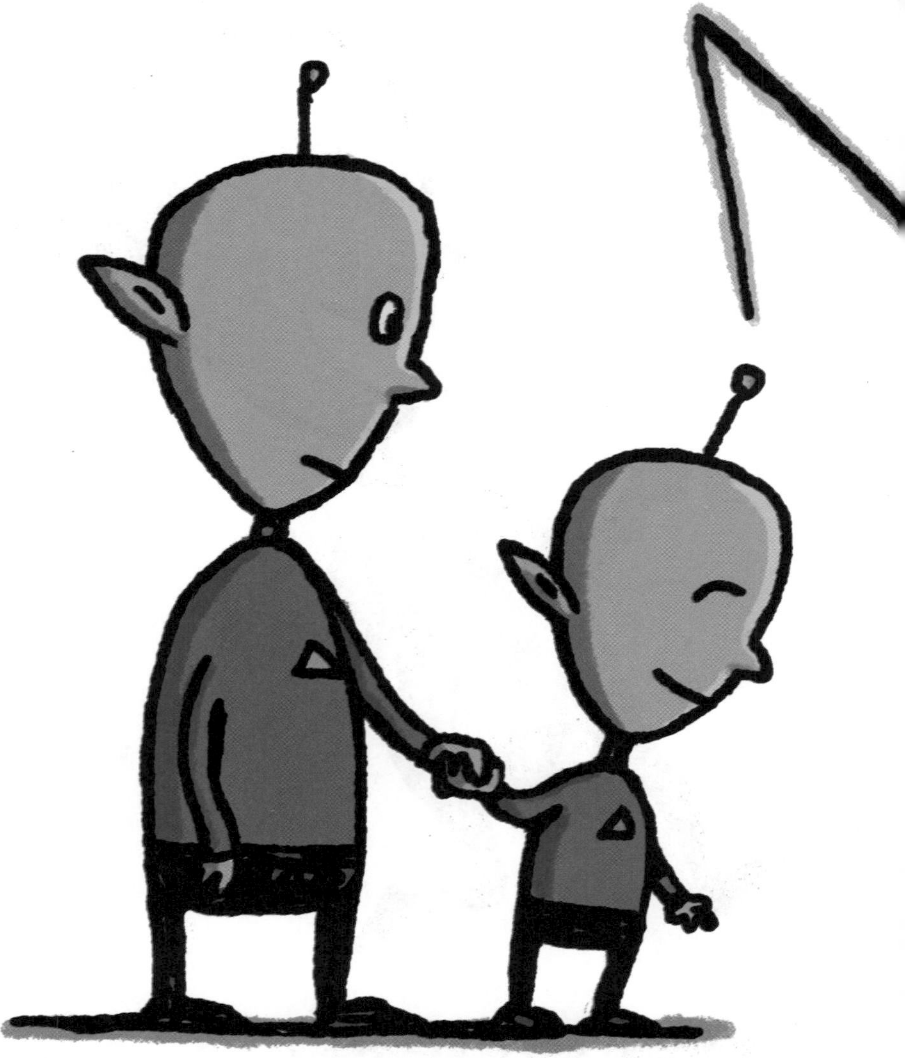

Zip zaps a car!

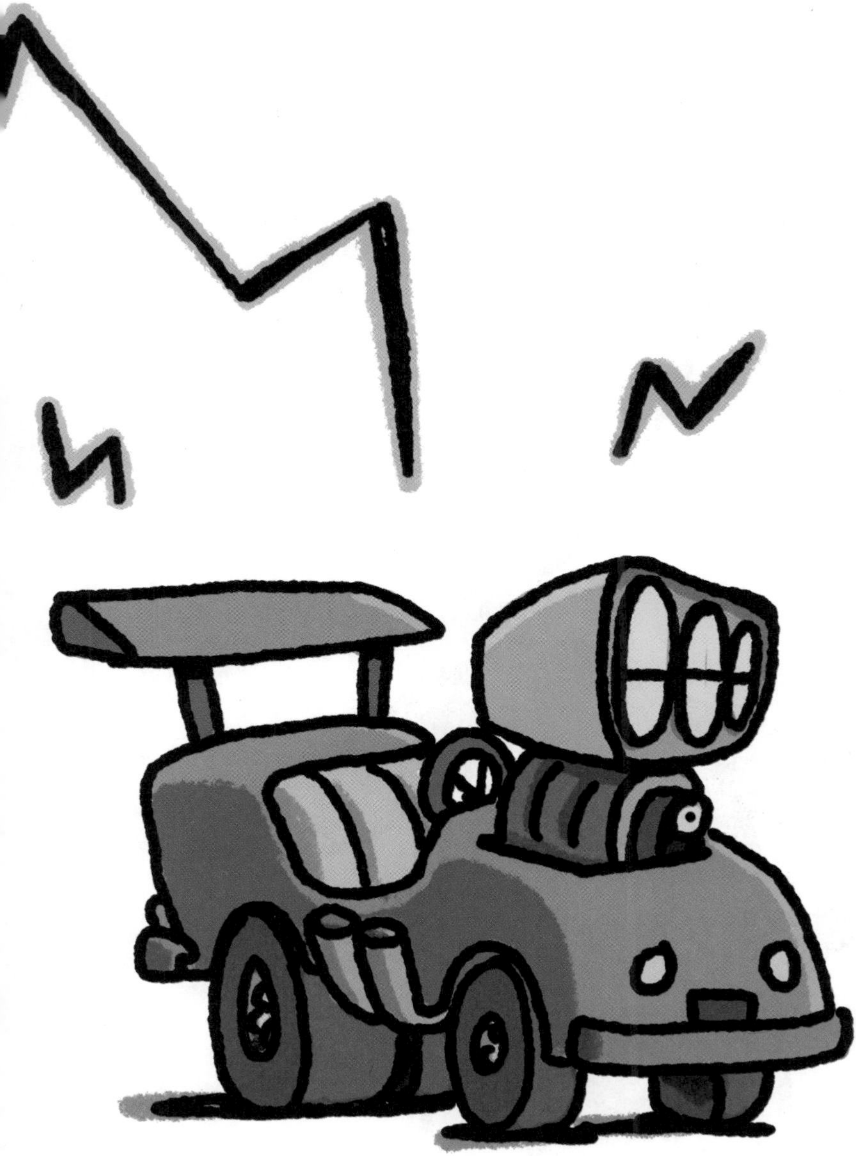

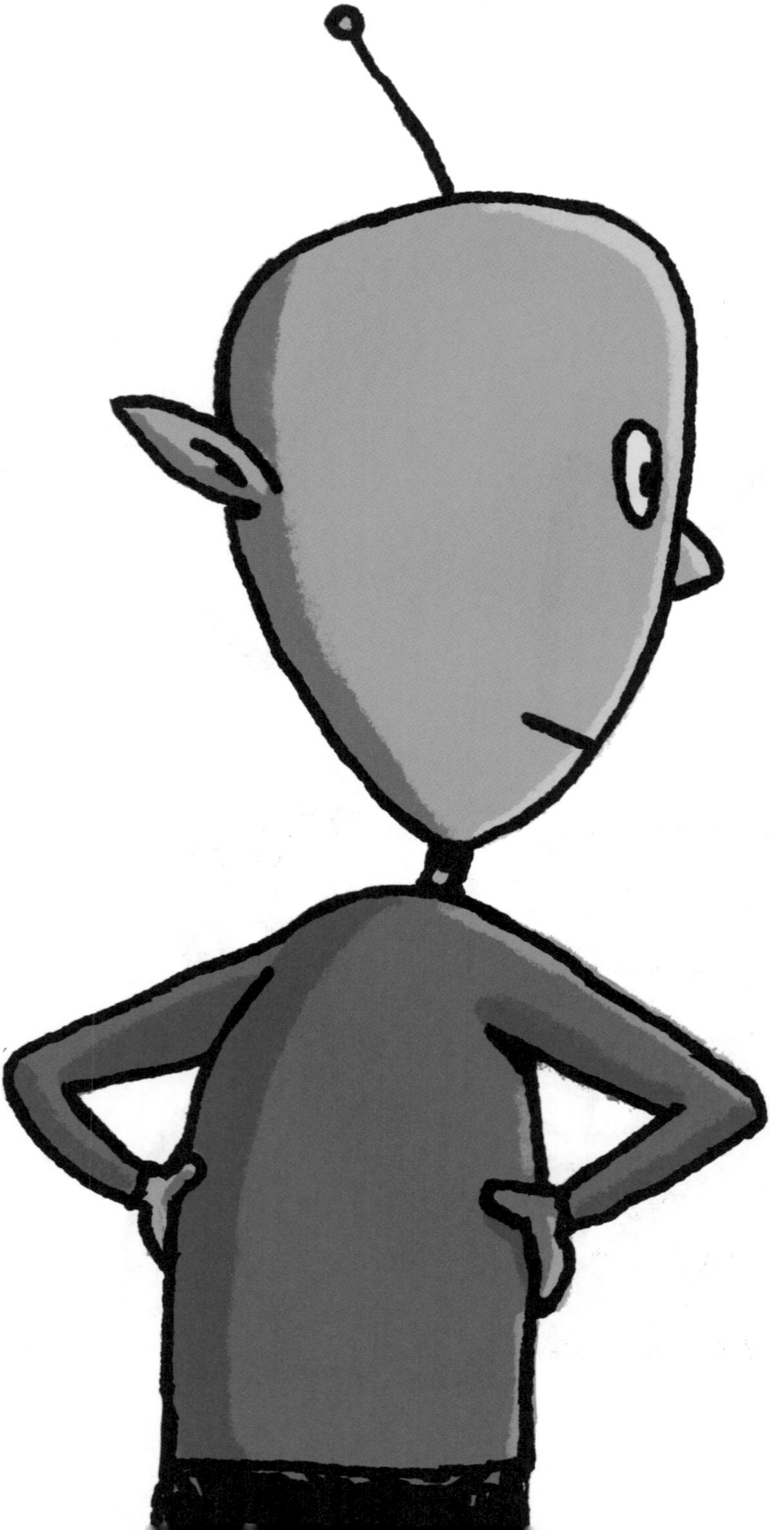

See Zip go.
Go fast and far.

"Not so fast,"
hear Zip's mom say.

"From me you cannot roll away."

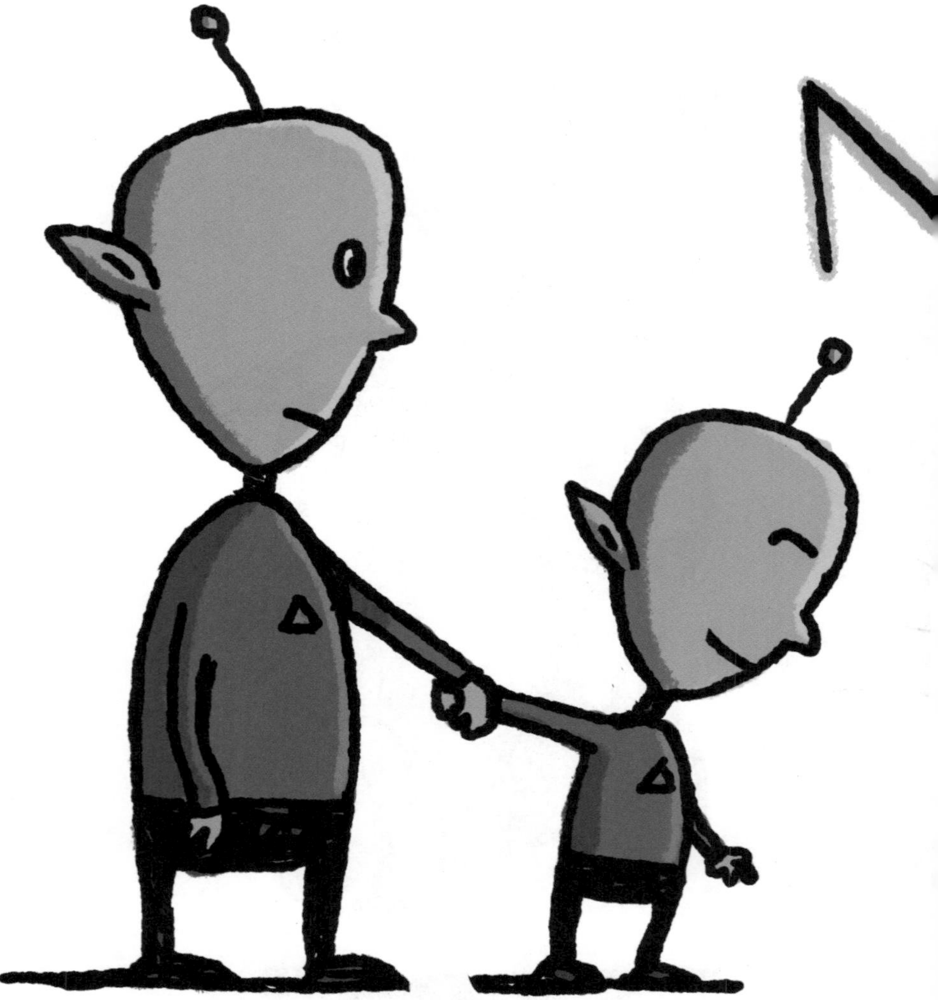

See Zip zap
a jet and go . . .

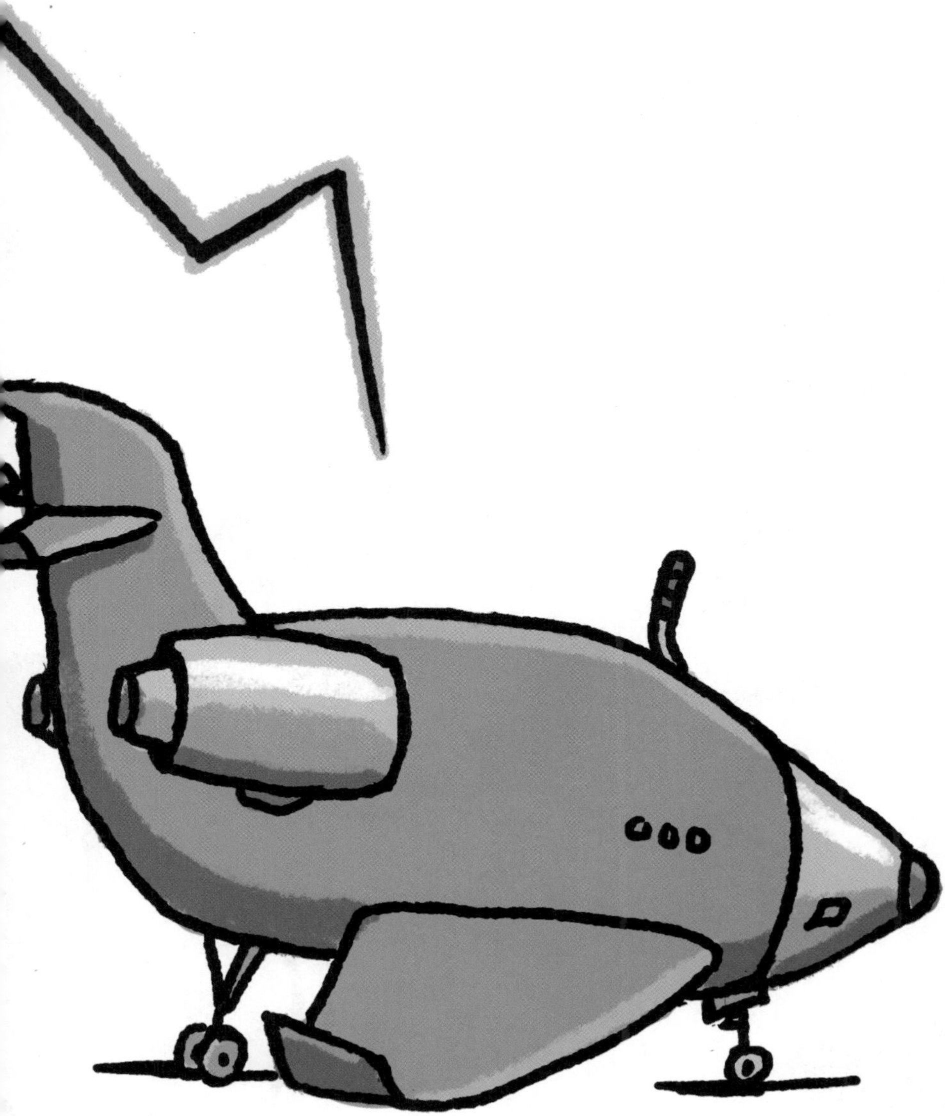

. . . faster than
the wind can blow.

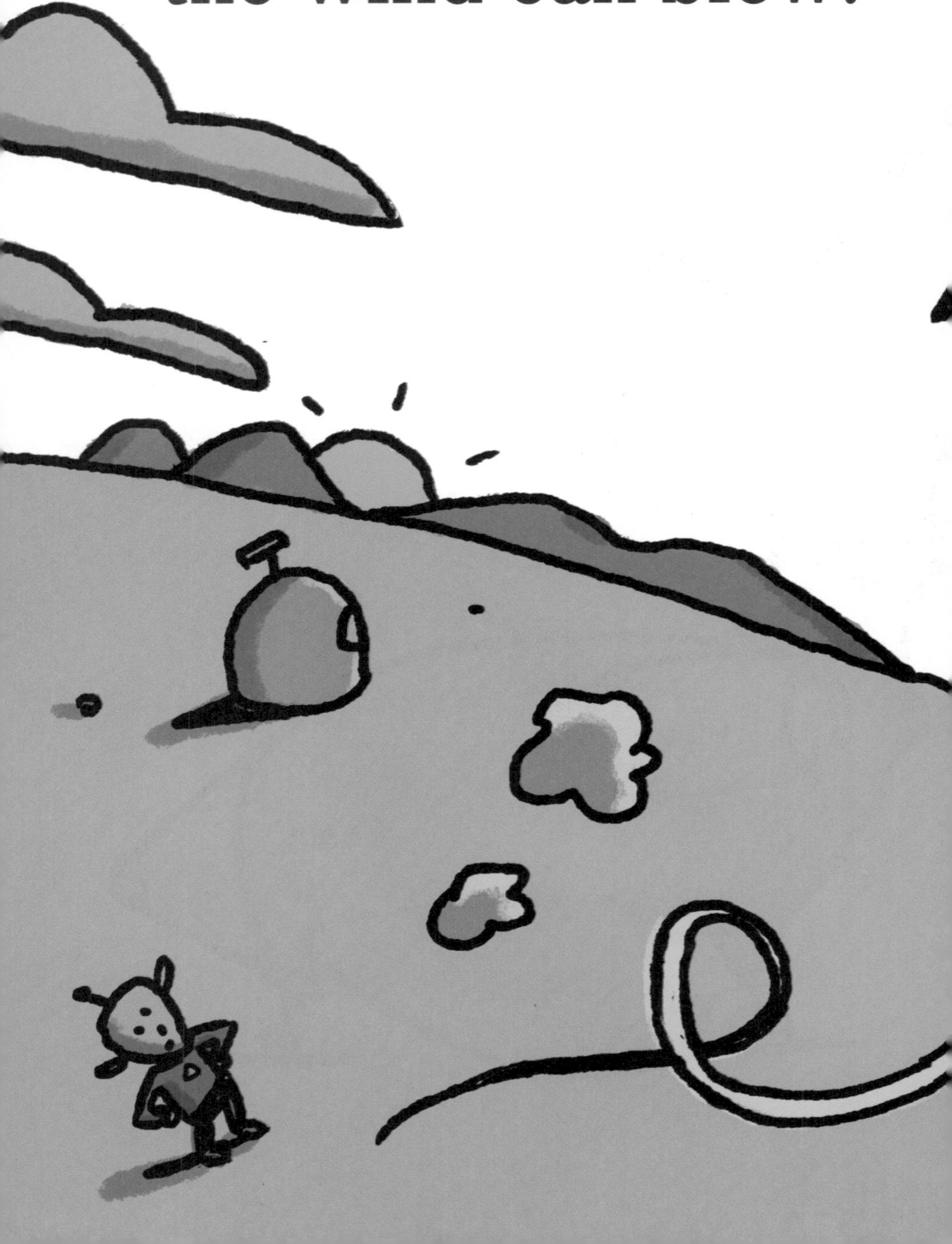

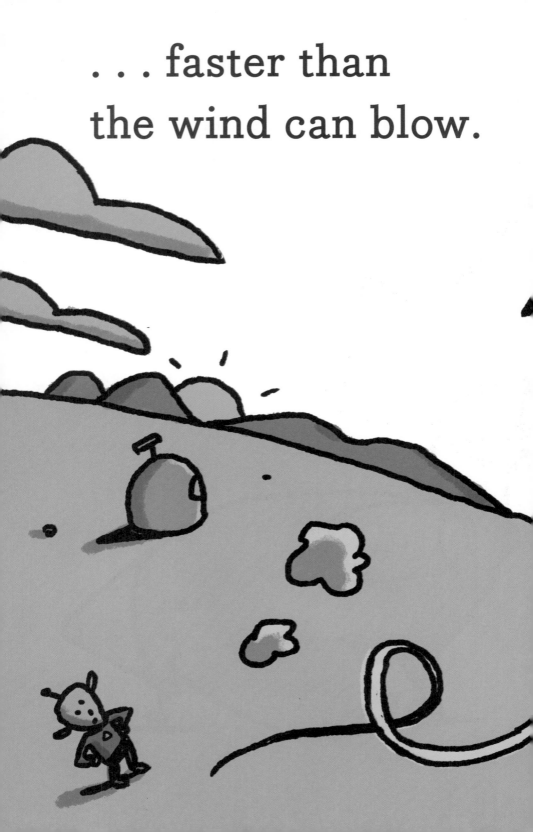

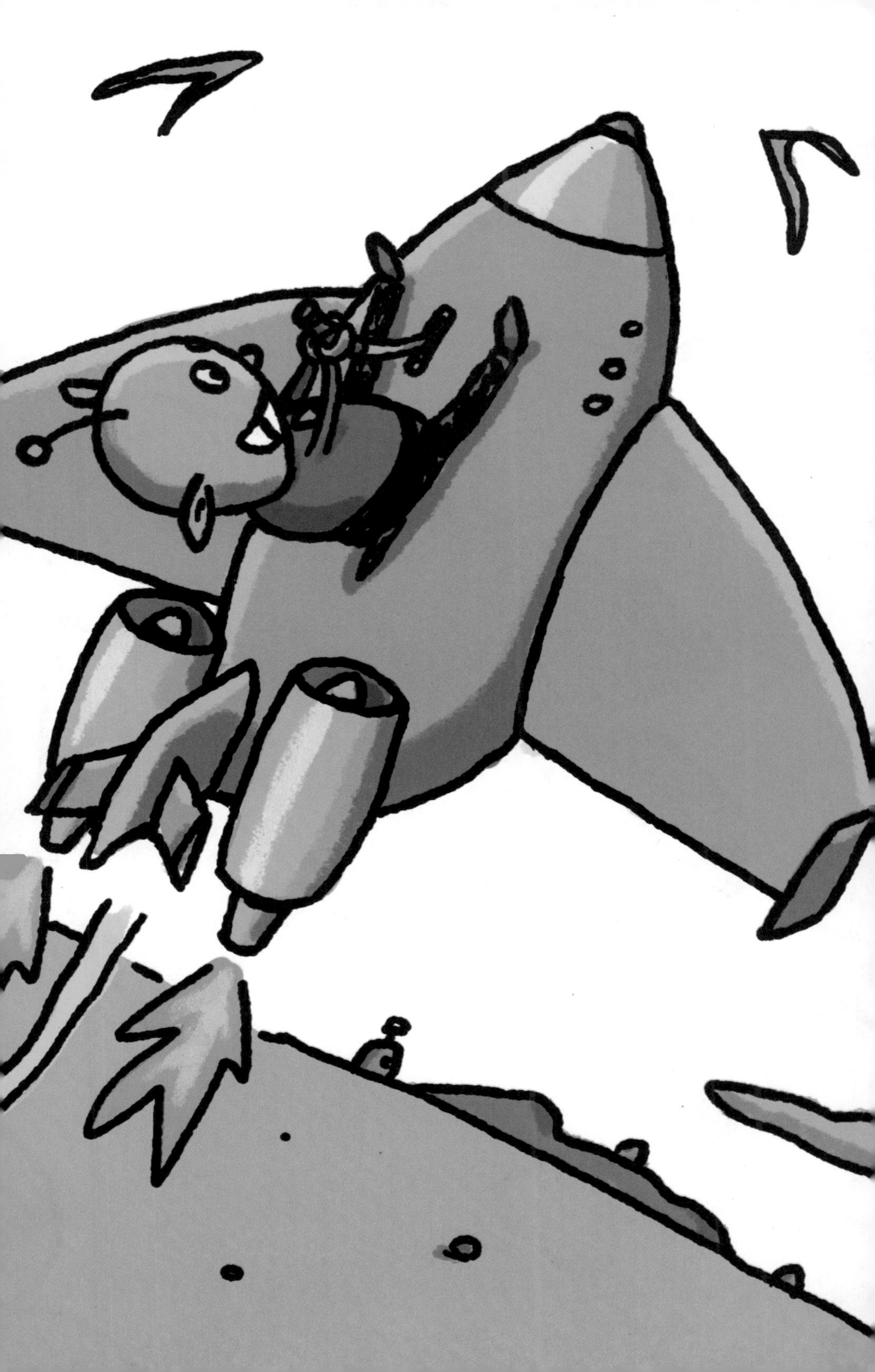

"Not so fast,"
hear Zip's mom say.

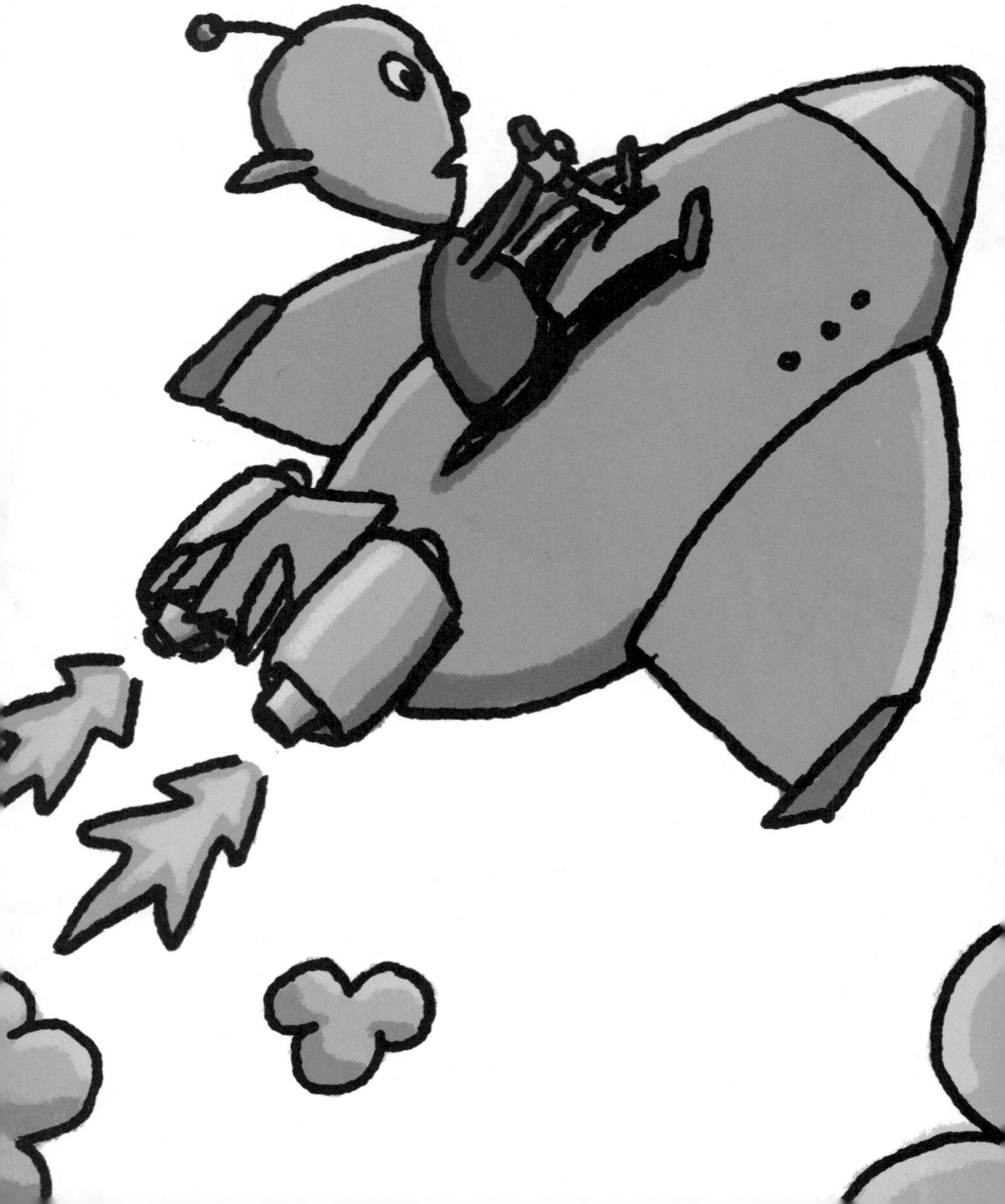

“From me you cannot fly away.

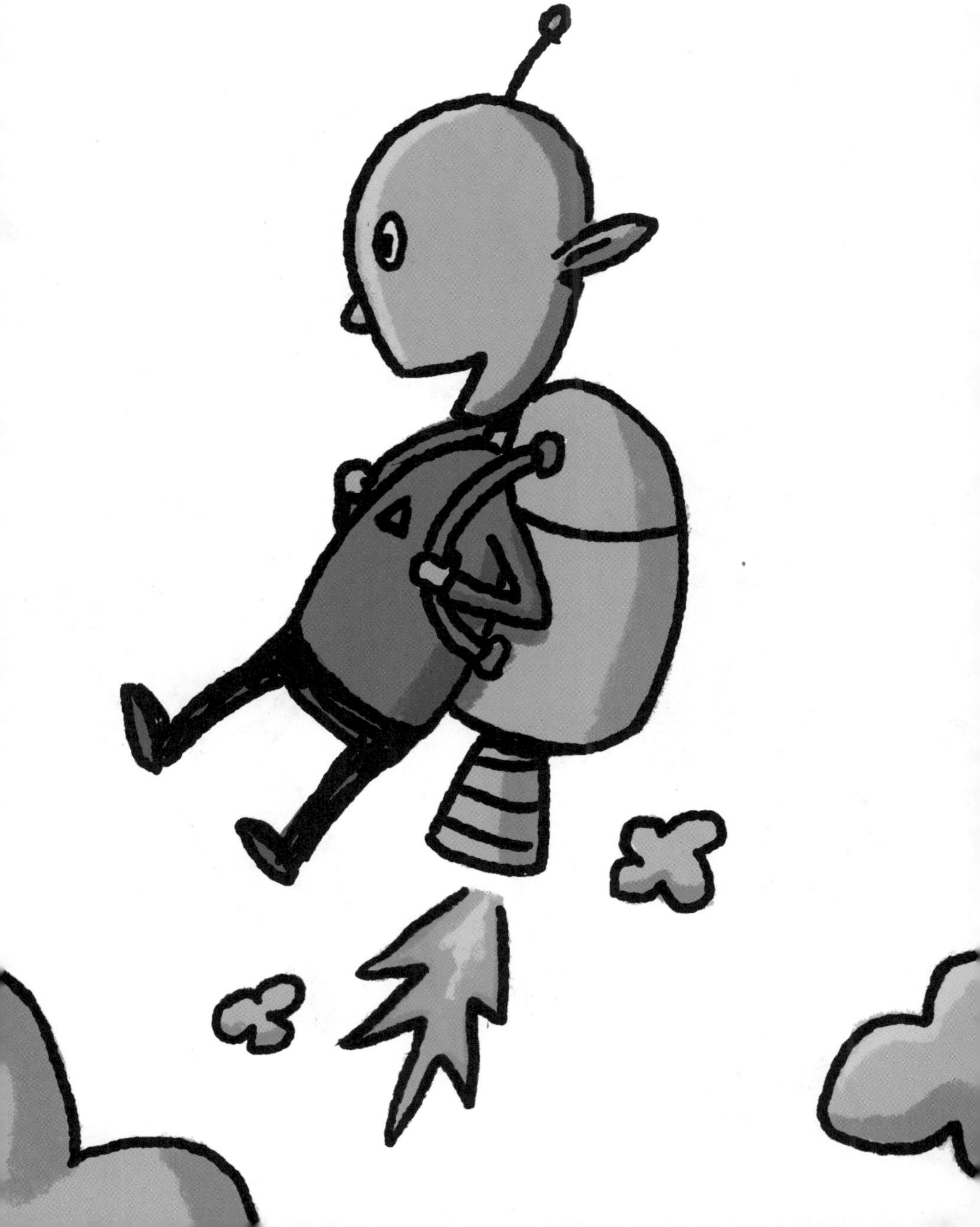

“You can zap,
fly, roll, and run,

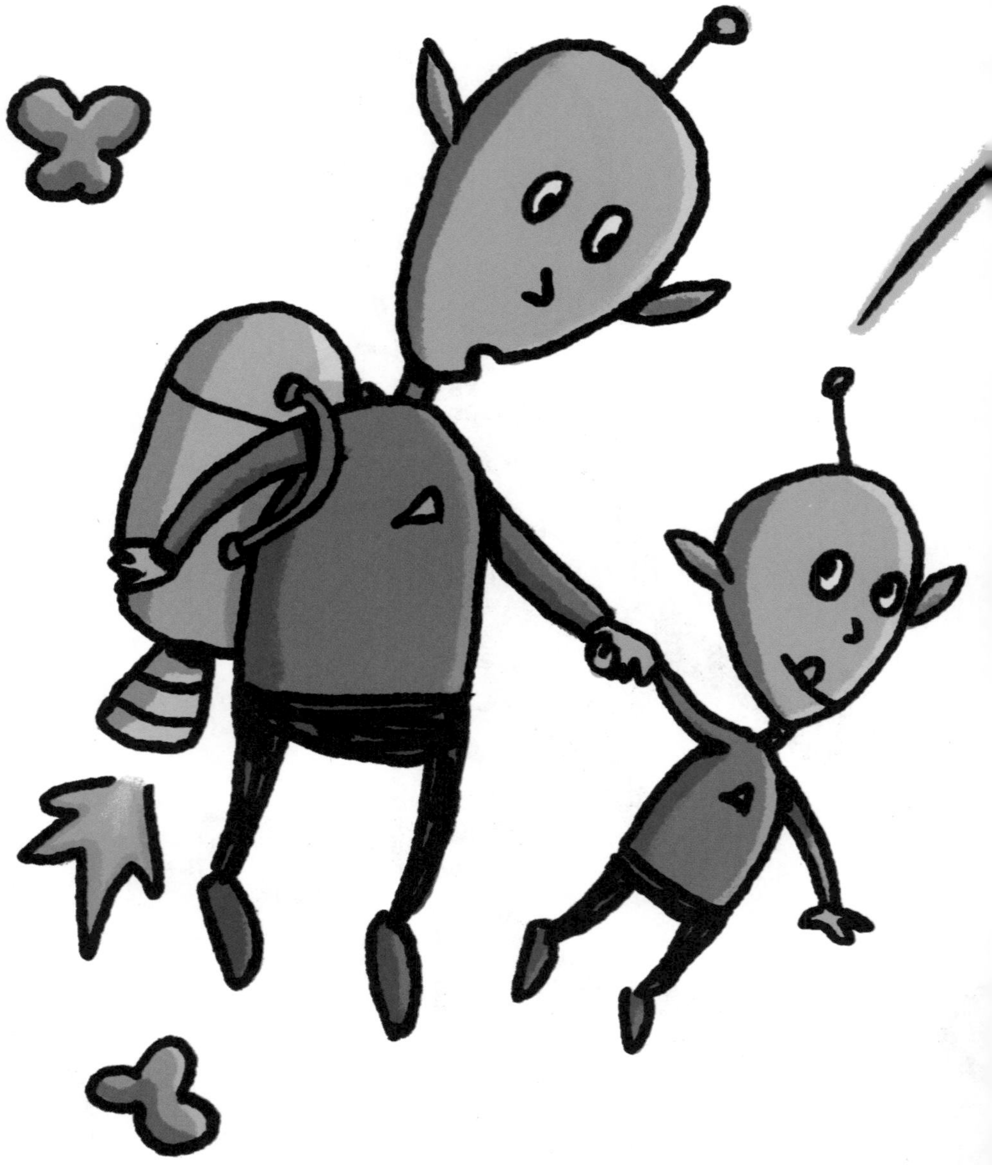

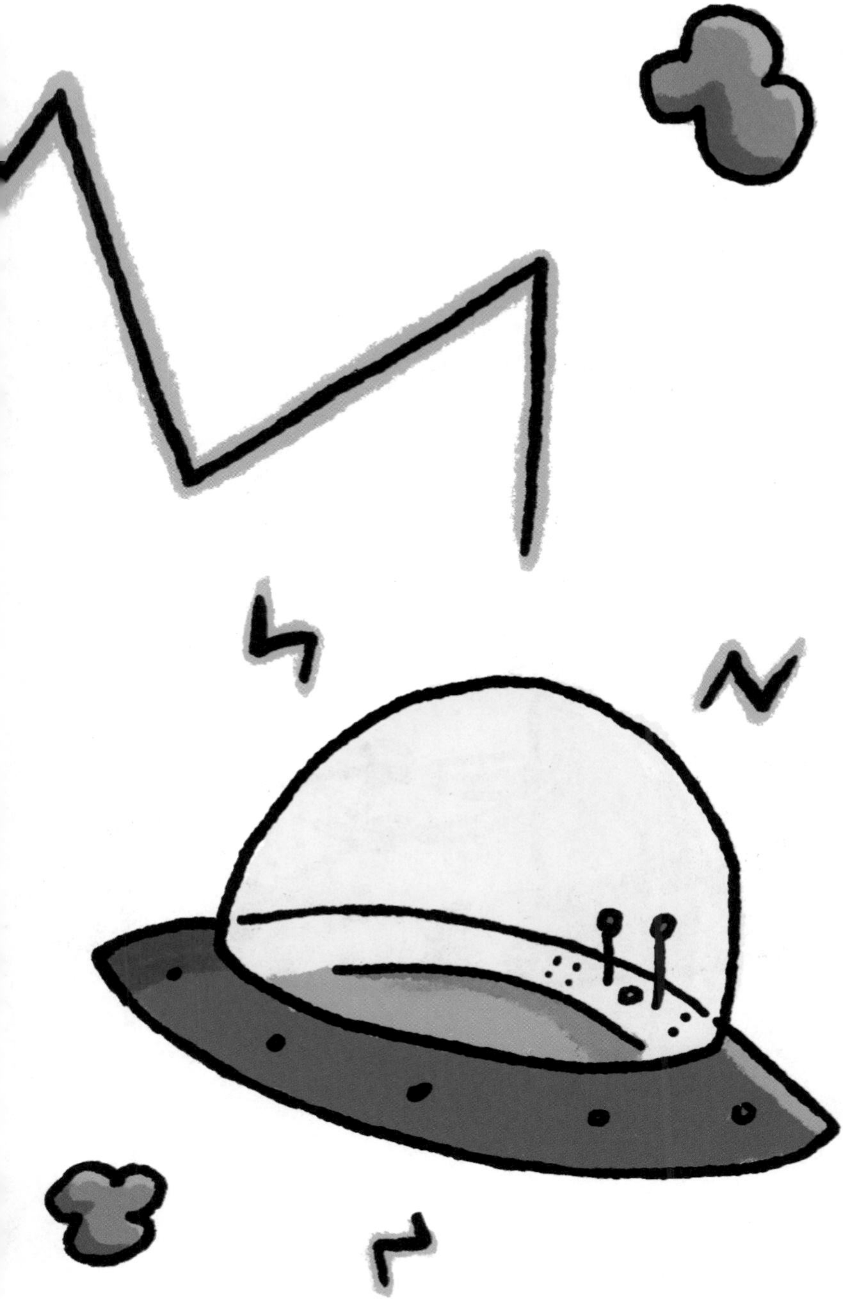

"and we can have
a bit more fun.

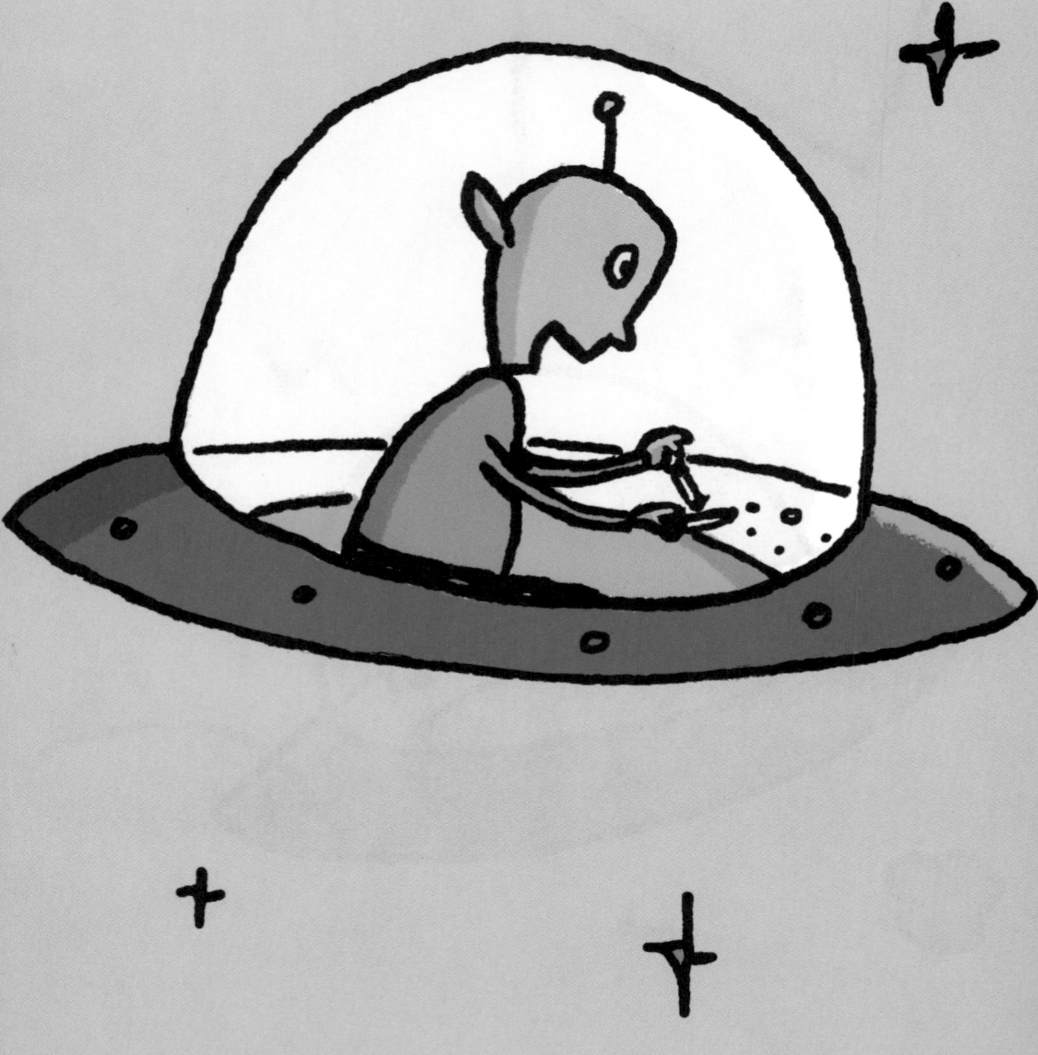

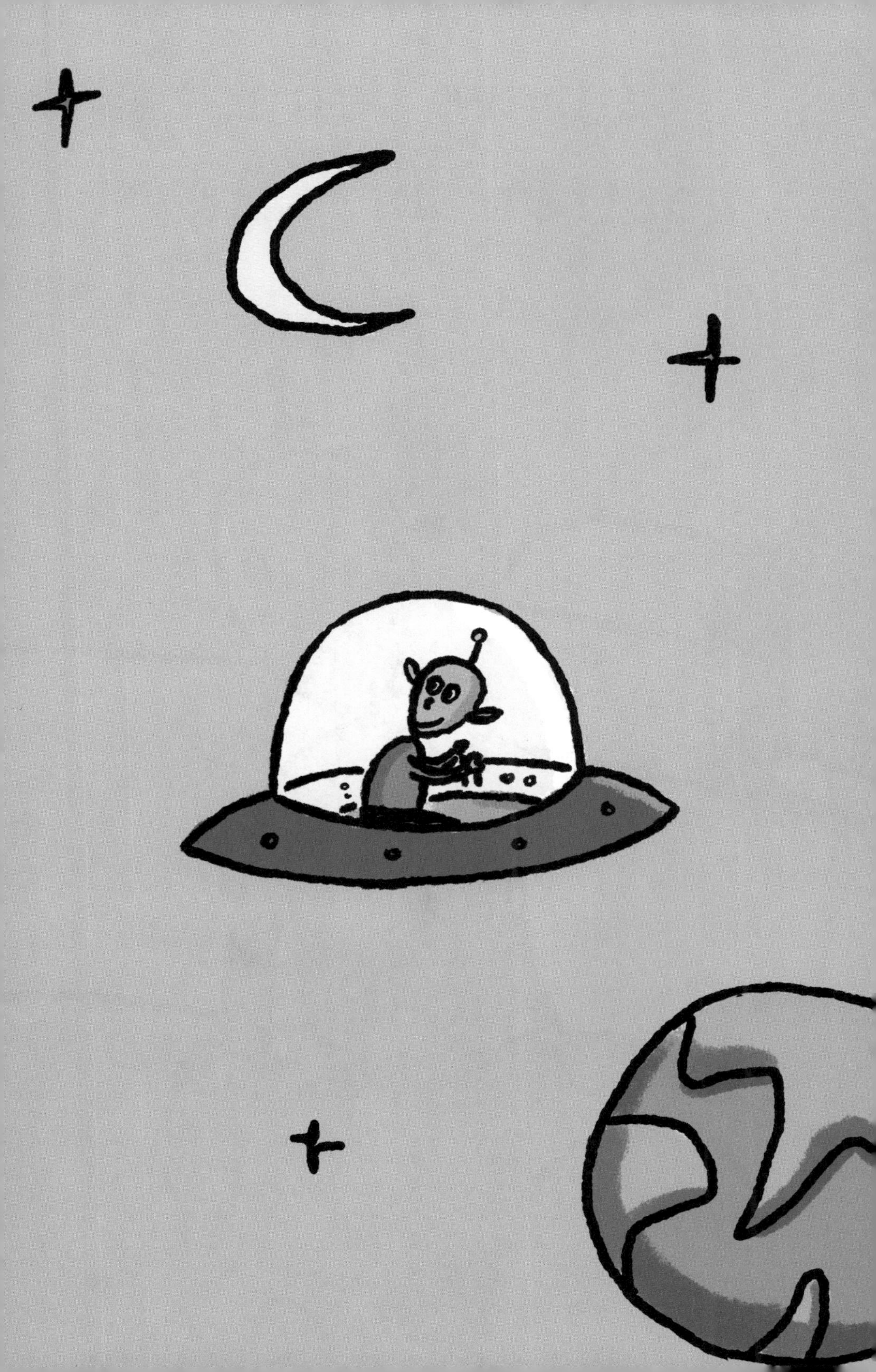

“But we cannot outrun the sun.

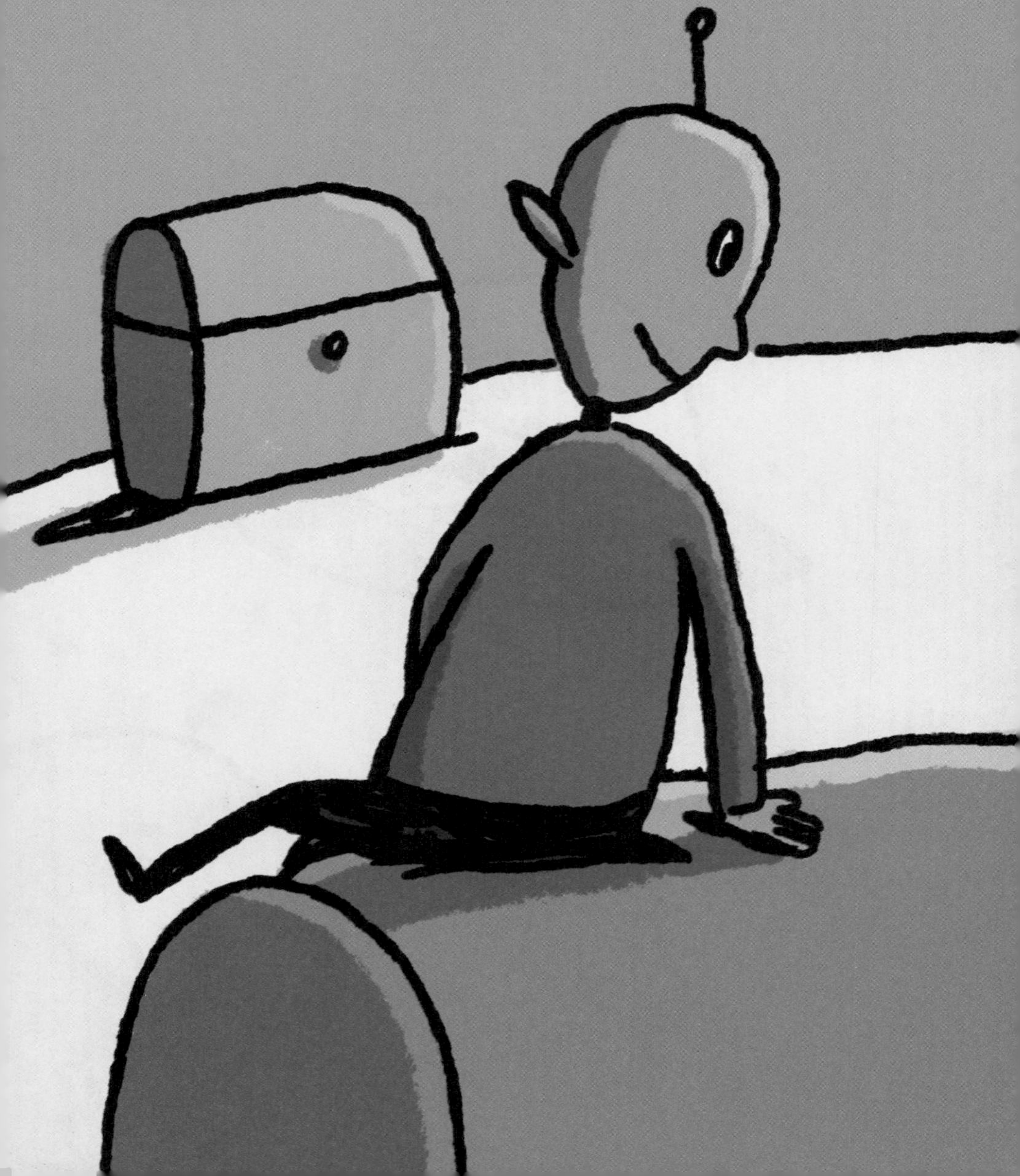

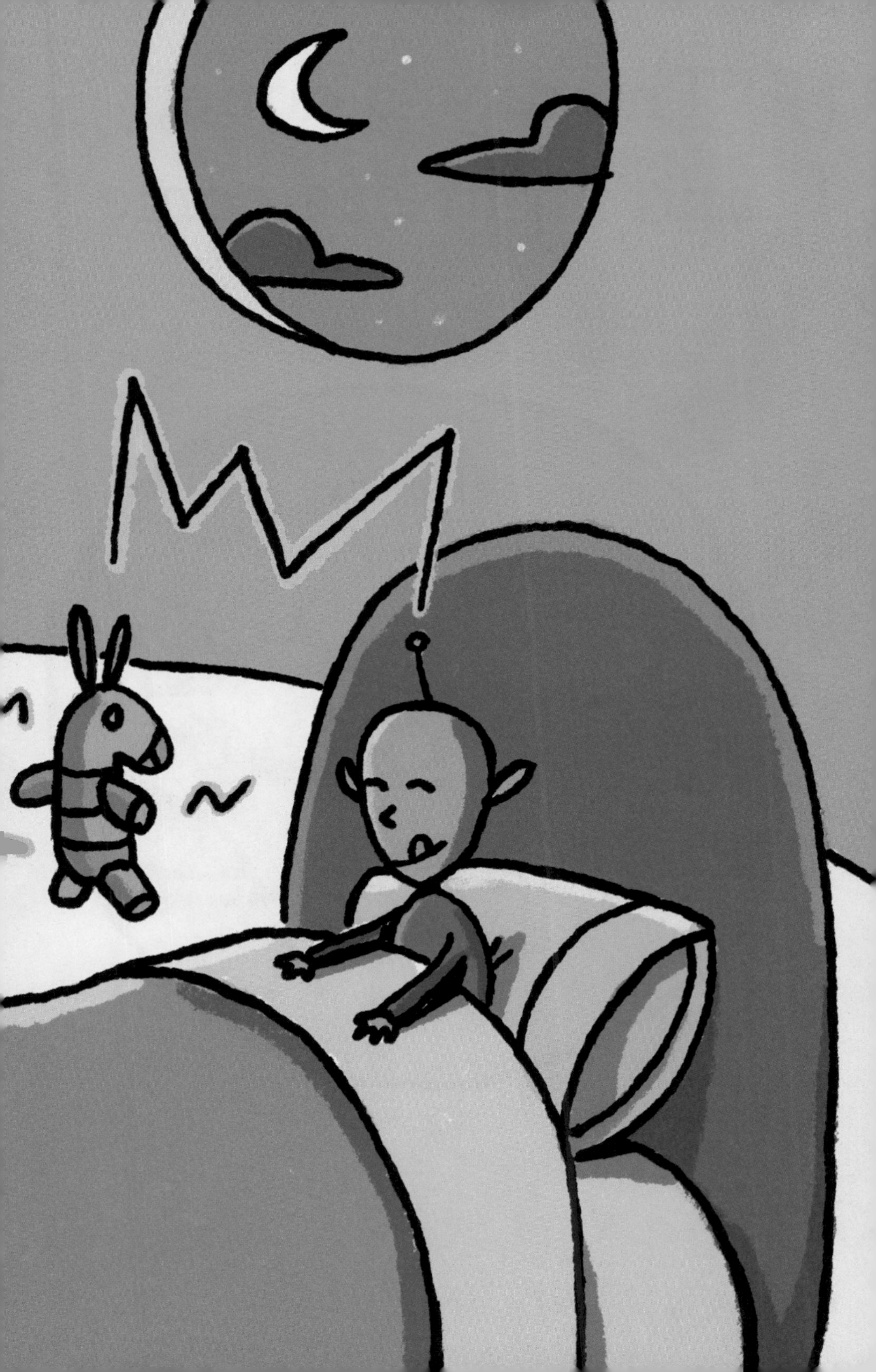

"The day is done,
and night has come."